Catch A
FIREFLY
and
Release A
DRAGON

Norm Richardson
Illustrated by Nicole Talbot

Copyright © 2014 by Norm Richardson. 141422-RICH

ISBN: Softcover   978-1-4931-6208-6
          EBook   978-1-4931-6209-3

This is a work of fiction. Names, characters, places and incidents either are the product of the author's imagination or are used fictitiously, and any resemblance to any actual persons, living or dead, events, or locales is entirely coincidental.

Rev. date: 01/17/2014

To order additional copies of this book, contact:
Xlibris LLC
1-888-795-4274
www.Xlibris.com
Orders@Xlibris.com

Dedication

To Mrs. Florence Clinton – Simpson, my 98 year old mother-in-law.

    Thanks for introducing my wife and I to South Florida and helping us feel so at home. It was here that I purchased the dragons, my inspiration for writing. Thanks for showing us your love in your own special way. Thanks for your encouragement, keeping me on task when all I wanted to do was go fishing.

    P. S. Can I go fishing now?   Please (smiles).

Norm

This adventure began in the small village of Chang Zhou, in the great country of China, with Yoyo and Khari Kambon. They had returned to their village after attending schools of higher learning. When they returned to the village, the village elders voted to make Yoyo the village accountant because of her ability to work with numbers and her bookkeeping skills. Khari was also voted in as one of the village caretakers because of his ability to draw and make signs. He also learned how to help manage the village very well. Working together, they became fond of one another. Khari proposed to Yoyo, she accepted, and they started their family.

They now had two very active children: a son, Kirin, who was ten, and a daughter, Yuanchu, who was eight. The children lovingly referred to their parents as Mamayo and Papari.

In the summer of the twenty-fifth year of the village, little Yuanchu sat on the side of the bed, gazing out of the bedroom window. "What are you staring at?" her brother, Kirin, asked.

As Yuanchu, with her bright eyes, turned to him, she had a big smile on her face. "Last night and the night before, I saw some very strange fireflies outside our neighbor's house."

"Do you mean Mr. Chinue's house?"

"Yes."

"Were they big ones?"

"No, just different."

Kirin had a questioning look on his face. "How were they different?"

"They flew in a circle, then flew away."

"You must have been dreaming, Yuanchu."

"No, I was wide awake, Kirin, honest."

"Go to sleep you two!"

"Yes, Mamayo, good night."

In a very soft voice Yuanchu whispered, "Let's just keep looking for a little while longer, Kirin, you'll see. OK?" And just then, in a short distance from their bedroom window, there appeared a line of fireflies that spun themselves into a circle and then took off in different directions. "You see, Kirin, I told you so."

Kirin swallowed deeply and couldn't speak for a moment. "Where did they go?"

"I don't know but they seemed to be in a hurry. Should we tell Mamayo and Papari?"

"No, let's try to catch one tomorrow night."

"What did you just ask me? Do you know that there are only three clear glass jars in this entire village? And you want me to lend you mine so you can fill it with fireflies?"

"Only one firefly, Mamayo, just one. Please? We'll wash it out before we give it back."

Mamayo looked down at little Yuanchu and said, "You are a strange one sometimes. Yes, you can borrow my clear jar but be very careful not to break it."

"Thank you, Mamayo, I love you, Mamayo."

Mamayo gave Yuanchu a big smile and said, "That's what family is about."

Yuanchu replied, "Yes, Mamayo."

That night Kirin made ready his butterfly net. He and Yuanchu waited outside their bedroom window in hopes that the strange fireflies would appear again. "I hope Mamayo and Papari don't catch us out here."

"Sshh, they will if you keep talking so loud."

And then all of a sudden they came, the strange fireflies, twelve in a roll, straight in a roll, and into a circle they went. Around and around they flew, and all of a sudden, puff, they spread out across the village, mingling in with the other fireflies. The children were so surprised, they didn't move at first, but then Kirin sprang into action, swinging his butterfly net through the air and running all around. Yuanchu just looked on in amazement.

Suddenly Kirin fell to the ground, breathing very hard. "I . . . I've got one, Yuanchu, I've got one."

"Don't squeeze it, you mustn't hurt it. Be very careful when you put it in the jar. There. Oh, Kirin, look at how beautiful it is."

"Look at all the colors."

"Let's show it to Mamayo."

"No, not tonight. Let's wait until tomorrow morning. We are supposed to be in bed."

Early the next morning Yuanchu rushed from the bedroom into the kitchen area, where Papari was having his morning meal. She grabbed him by his hand. "Come, Papari, and see our beautiful firefly."

"What is it, my daughter?"

"Our firefly we caught last night."

"When you were supposed to be in bed?" Yuanchu looked up at Papari with a look of surprise on her face. "Your mother and I heard the two of you outside last night. So that's what you were up to, catching fireflies?"

"Yes, Papari, please come and see our beautiful firefly."

When they went into the bedroom (with Yuanchu pulling Papari along), Kirin was still lying in bed, still exhausted from his great chase last night. On a small table in the corner of the small room was Mamayo's clear glass jar, and in it was the most beautiful firefly Papari had ever seen. As he stared at it, a big smile came to his face, and he turned to look down at Yuanchu. "Where did this firefly come from?"

Kirin spoke up as he sat up in bed. "From over by Mr. Chinue's house. He has lots of them."

"Good morning, my son."

"Good morning, Papari. Just wait until Mamayo sees this thing."

"You two get washed up for your morning meal."

As the children sat down for their morning tea and marmalade bread, Mamayo asked them about their adventure outside last night. "We caught the most beautiful firefly, didn't we, Papari?"

"Yes, you did, Yuanchu."

"And you put it in my clear glass jar?"

"Yes, Mamayo." Yuanchu smiled.

Mamayo looked over at Papari. "What are we going to do with them?"

They both just smiled.

When the children returned to their bedroom after the morning meal, they went straight to the jar to look at the firefly again. Kirin asked Yuanchu, "What should we do with him?"

As they stared at it, its wings began to flutter very fast just like hummingbird wings, then they stopped. "I'm not a firefly!"

The children looked at one another. "Did you hear that?"

"I think so. He said he wasn't a firefly."

"And I'm not a he!"

Yuanchu jumped up and started to run from the bedroom. "I'm going to tell Mamayo right now!"

"Wait, Yuanchu, let's wait and see if he says anything else."

"I'M NOT A HE!"

The children just looked at one another in total shock. Kirin spoke up. "Who are you?"

"My name is Teapot. I'm not a he, I'm a she. And I'm not a firefly. Would you like to see what I really am?"

The children looked at each other once again and then back at Teapot. "Yes."

Teapot started to flap her wings very, very fast and then they stopped. Her body began to glow with the most beautiful colors. Beautiful blues and greens, wonderful yellows and purples, and the brightest reds and lavenders the children had ever seen. They could only look at Teapot in amazement. When Kirin turned to speak with Yuanchu, she was already running to tell Mamayo, and as he glanced back at the jar, he's frozen with shock as he saw something he'd never seen before—a very small dragon, but he didn't know what it was.

Yuanchu was now pulling Mamayo into the bedroom to see the firefly. "I've seen enough bugs in my life. What's so special about this one?" As Mamayo gazed into the jar, she too was amazed by all the brilliant colors, but she only saw a firefly, not a small dragon as the children did. "Oh, this bug is very pretty."

"Don't you see, Mamayo? Don't you see it's different from the others?"

"Yes, the colors are very bright, but I have work to do, so you two enjoy your bug. I must start my work." And off she went, back to the kitchen area.

"Why can't our parents see you for what you really are?"

Teapot revved her wings just slightly and spoke. "They are too old. They have lost their childhood innocence. Only the young children like yourselves can see us for what we really are."

"How many of you are there?" Yuanchu asked.

With wings revving ever so slightly, Teapot answered, "There are twelve of us in this village. I will tell you things you may not understand right now, but later in your life you will. I'm in this village to do one certain mission and that is to gather up all the arguments I can find."

The children looked at each other with questioning looks on their faces. Kirin spoke up. "What do you mean, Teapot? If that is your name."

Teapot blinked her sleepy eyes at them. "I'm only here to help in keeping the village safe and happy. I only try to remove arguments. I breathe them in as you breathe in air. They leave my body as rainbow colors through my skin. You know there are other problems in this village and all over this great country and all over this world, but I do my part in this village."

Yuanchu spoke up. "Please tell me again what you do."

"I will tell you once again. When people get upset with one another, I make the arguments go away. You must release me now so I can continue my mission!"

"But why?" Yuanchu asked.

"This is the year of the dragon. In thirteen days I will not have enough strength left to complete my task if I'm still in this jar. There are no arguments in this house for me to gather. You must release me so I can continue my mission!"

Kirin spoke. "How do we know you are telling the truth?"

Once again teapot revved up her wings and started to glow with her beautiful colors more brilliant than ever before. "I will barter with you for my freedom. I will grant the two of you three wishes, and in return, you must promise to let me go. Do you promise?"

They looked at each other, and at the same time, they said yes.

"Think well of what you might desire before you ask of it. Once you have asked of it, only that will be done. Think of your family and not only of yourselves. Think hard, young ones."

Yuanchu spoke first, and with a big smile, she said, "I wish to be a great dancer."

"Done!" Teapot answered.

Kirin spoke up. "Yuanchu, you have spoken too fast! One wish is used. We should have asked Mamayo and Papari first."

"Think hard, young ones," spoke Teapot, "you have two wishes."

The children retreated to the kitchen area, where their parents were, and sat down quietly. "Now what are you two up to?" Mamayo asked.

Yuanchu looked up at Papari. "What would you wish for?"

"What do you mean, Yuanchu?"

"If you could wish for anything, what would you wish for, Papari?"

Papari looked over at his two beautiful children and said, "Once a wise man traveled to our village, and people would stop to listen to him speak in the early evenings. He always spoke about family. He once said to us,

The family that catches the first rays of sun together,

The family that prays together,

The family that plays together

And spends the most time together,

They find ways together

To stay together

As a close family should.

"With all the sincerity in my heart, I want us to remain the closest family in our village. This is our mission, to teach the two of you that family comes first before anything else. You will be good thinkers and problem solvers because we will teach you by our examples, and we will teach you right from wrong so that you will make good life decisions. That's what I would wish for."

The children jumped from their chairs and ran back into their bedroom.

Mamayo looked lovingly at Papari. "That was a very inspiring and thoughtful message you gave to them."

"We must always remember to teach them—family first."

The children once again sat down on the floor in front of the glass jar and stared at Teapot as she stared back at them. "What are your other wishes? You have two more."

Kirin looked over to his sister and said, "Our parents want us to be the most loving and caring family in the village, and so do we. We wish for that, don't we, Yuanchu?"

"Yes, we do."

"Done!" Teapot declared. "And what will be your last wish?"

Kirin looked into the jar and said, "I would like very much to be able to play the flute and I wish for that."

"Done!" once again Teapot proclaimed. "And now you must release me as you have promised to do."

The children looked at one another sadly. "Teapot, do we have to let you go right now?"

"If you want your wishes to come true, *yes*. Don't be sad! Just release me. As I fly away from you and the space between us grows, your memory of me will fade away also, and I will grant the wishes you have requested. Keep your promise, and open the jar."

As Yuanchu slowly opened the jar, Teapot immediately flew out and beamed with other brilliant colors she had not shown them before and gave out a warm hum of satisfaction as she dashed to the ceiling of the room. The children looked very sad as she slowly moved toward the window and spoke to them for the very last time. "Farewell, young ones. In all that you pursue in life, my wish for you is to fare well." And then out the window she flew, never to be seen by the children again. They ran into the kitchen area to tell Papari they released their firefly.

"I'm very proud of both of you. You have given the firefly more days of life. That was a good decision the two of you made."

The next day the family went on their weekly trip to the village market to buy fresh food for the coming week. A large number of the villagers were already there, buying and selling many different items. The children were allowed to go and mingle with friends from school while their parents did some of the shopping.

As Kirin passed Mr. Chinue's (his neighbor) chair stand, he stopped to say good-day to him, and Mr. Chinue handed Kirin a bamboo flute, and with a smile he said, "I think you might like this."

Kirin was surprised. He thanked Mr. Chinue and ran to ask Papari if he could keep the flute. And Papari agreed. "It's OK."

As the children reunited with their school friends, they noticed some older students not too far from them dancing to music being played by some of the village elders, and they decided to join in the fun. Yuanchu immediately picked up the music rhythm and started to dance with her hands in a circle above her head and her toes pointed away from her. The people watching were amazed at how a small child could be so gifted with dance abilities, and they looked at Mamayo with smiles of approval. One of the elders playing the music motioned to Kirin and one of his friends to stand beside him and play the flutes that Mr. Chinue gave them, which they did (not very well at first, but they were encouraged to keep trying). The more they played, the better they sounded.

Papari was so proud of his children. One of his coworkers who was also off for the day commented to him how just yesterday, so many villagers seemed to be so upset with one another at the market, and today most of them seemed to be so pleasant.

Summer into fall, fall into winter, winter into spring, and spring into summer again. The years passed and the children, now young adults, had no memory of their encounter with Teapot the dragon, but they did remember and cherish the life lessons that their parents taught them about family. They were happy to have been raised in such a peaceful village. Yuanchu went on to become a very popular dancer and lived a very happy and rewarding life, passing on the good family values taught to her, as did Kirin, who now played his flute at the market with the elders whenever he got an opportunity to.

The wise man once said: Patience and communication are keys for young people to succeed. They will listen to their parents when their parents listen to them.

The End.

Edwards Brothers Malloy
Thorofare, NJ USA
September 19, 2016